PUFFIN CLASSICS

OUR EXPLOITS AT WEST POLEY

When Leonard arrives for a holiday on his cousin Steve's farm, he is disappointed to find that the Mendip Hills are not as high as he had hoped. But danger and excitement await *inside* the hills, and soon the two boys are exploring the local caves. Imagine their excitement when they stumble across an undergound river whose course they can divert . . . especially when they realize this is the river that runs through the local village!

Thomas Hardy was born in Dorset in 1840. He trained as an architect but began to publish novels in the early 1870s. *Our Exploits at West Poley*, the only children's story he wrote, was commissioned by an American journal and first published in 1891–2, at the height of Hardy's fame. He died in 1928, recognized as one of the masters of the English novel.

Thomas Hardy

OUR EXPLOITS AT WEST POLEY

Illustrated by Alexy Pendle

PUFFIN BOOKS

Puffin Books, Penguin Books Ltd, Harmondsworth, Middlesex, England
Penguin Books Ltd, Harmondsworth, Middlesex, England
Penguin Books, 625 Madison Avenue, New York, New York 10022, U.S.A.
Penguin Books Australia Ltd, Ringwood, Victoria, Australia
Penguin Books Canada Ltd, 2801 John Street, Markham, Ontario, Canada L3R 1B4
Penguin Books (N.Z.) Ltd, 182–190 Wairau Road, Auckland 10, New Zealand

First published in serial form in *The Household*, November 1892–April 1893
Published in Puffin Books 1983

Made and printed in Great Britain by
Cox & Wyman Ltd, Reading
Set in Linotron Palatino by
Rowland Phototypesetting Ltd,
Bury St Edmunds, Suffolk

CONTENTS

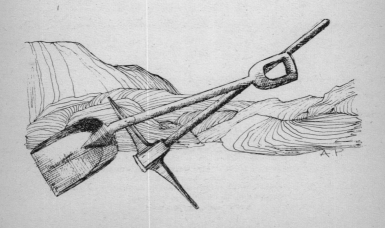

CHAPTER
1

HOW WE WENT EXPLORING
UNDERGROUND

. . . I seem to hear the pattering of that mill-wheel when
we walked by it, as well as if it were going now . . .

On a certain fine evening of early autumn – I will not say how many years ago – I alighted from a green gig, before the door of a farmhouse at West Poley, a village in Somersetshire. I had reached the age of thirteen, and though rather small for my age, I was robust and active. My father was a schoolmaster, living about twenty miles off. I had arrived on a visit to my Aunt Draycot, a farmer's widow, who, with her son Stephen, or Steve, as he was invariably called by his friends, still managed the farm, which had been left on her hands by her deceased husband.

Steve promptly came out to welcome me. He was two or three years my senior, tall, lithe, ruddy, and somewhat masterful withal. There was that force about him which was less suggestive of intellectual power than (as

Carlyle said of Cromwell) 'Doughtiness – the courage and faculty to do.'

When the first greetings were over, he informed me that his mother was not indoors just then, but that she would soon be home. 'And, do you know, Leonard,' he continued, rather mournfully, 'she wants me to be a farmer all my life, like my father.'

'And why not be a farmer all your life, like your father?' said a voice behind us.

We turned our heads, and a thoughtful man in a threadbare, yet well-fitting suit of clothes, stood near, as he paused for a moment on his way down to the village.

'The straight course is generally the best for boys,' the speaker continued, with a smile. 'Be sure that professions you know little of have as many drudgeries attaching to them as those you know well – it is only their remoteness that lends them their charm.' Saying this he nodded and went on.

'Who is he?' I asked.

'Oh – he's nobody,' said Steve. 'He's a man who has been all over the world, and tried all sorts of lives, but he has never got rich, and now he has retired to this place for quietness. He calls himself the Man who has Failed.'

After this explanation I thought no more of the Man who had Failed than Steve himself did; neither of us was at that time old enough to know that the losers in the world's battle are often the very men who, too late for themselves, have the clearest perception of what constitutes success; while the successful men are frequently blinded to the same by the tumult of their own progress.

To change the subject, I said something about the village and Steve's farmhouse – that I was glad to see the latter was close under the hills, which I hoped we might climb before I returned home. I had expected to find these hills much higher, and I told Steve so without disguise.

'They may not be very high, but there's a good deal inside 'em,' said my cousin as we entered the house, as if he thought me hypercritical, 'a good deal more than you think.'

'Inside 'em?' said I. 'Stone and earth, I suppose.'

'More than that,' said he. 'You have heard of the Mendip Caves, haven't you?'

'But they are nearer Cheddar,' I said.

'There are one or two in this place, likewise,' Steve

answered me. 'I can show them to you tomorrow. People say there are many more, only there is no way of getting into them.'

Being disappointed in the height of the hills, I was rather incredulous about the number of the caves; but on my saying so, Steve rejoined, 'Whatever you may think, I went the other day into one of 'em – Nick's Pocket – that's the cavern nearest here, and found that what was called the end was not really the end at all. Ever since then I've wanted to be an explorer, and not a farmer; and in spite of that old man, I think I am right.'

At this moment my aunt came in, and soon after we were summoned to supper; and during the remainder of the evening nothing more was said about the Mendip Caves. It would have been just as well for us two boys if nothing more had been said about them at all; but it was fated to be otherwise, as I have reason to remember.

Steve did not forget my remarks, which, to him, no doubt, seemed to show a want of appreciation for the features of his native district. The next morning he returned to the subject, saying, as he came indoors to me suddenly, 'I mean to show ye a little of what the Mendips contain, Leonard, if you'll come with me. But we must go quietly, for my mother does not like me to prowl about such places, because I get muddy. Come here, and see the preparations I have made.'

He took me into the stable, and showed me a goodly supply of loose candle ends; also a bit of board perforated with holes, into which the candles would fit, and shaped to a handle at one extremity. He had provided, too, some slices of bread and cheese, and several apples. I was at once convinced that caverns which demanded such preparations must be something larger than the mere gravel-pits I had imagined; but I said nothing beyond assenting to the excursion.

It being the time after harvest, while there was not much to be attended to on the farm, Steve's mother could easily spare him, 'to show me the neighbourhood', as he expressed it, and off we went, with our provisions and candles.

A quarter of a mile, or possibly a little more – for my recollections on matters of distance are not precise – brought us to the mouth of the cave called Nick's Pocket, the way thither being past the village houses, and the mill, and across the mill-stream, which came from a copious spring in the hillside some distance farther up. I seem to hear the pattering of that mill-wheel when we walked by it, as well as if it were going now; and yet how many years have passed since the sound beat last upon my ears.

The mouth of the cave was screened by bushes, the face of the hill behind being, to the best of my remembrance, almost vertical. The spot was obviously well known to the inhabitants, and was the haunt of many boys, as I could see by footprints; though the cave, at this time, with others thereabouts, had been but little examined by tourists and men of science.

We entered unobserved, and no sooner were we inside, than Steve lit a couple of candles and stuck them into the board. With these he showed the way. We

walked on over a somewhat uneven floor, the novelty of
the proceeding impressing me, at first, very agreeably;
the light of the candles was sufficient, at first, to reveal
only the nearer stalactites, remote nooks of the cavern
being left in well-nigh their original, mystic shadows.
Steve would occasionally turn, and accuse me, in arch
tones, of being afraid, which accusation I (as a boy would
naturally do) steadfastly denied; though even now I can
recollect that I experienced more than once some sort of
misgiving.

'As for me – I have been there hundreds of times,'
Steve said proudly. 'We West Poley boys come here
continually to play "I spy", and think nothing of running
in with no light of any sort. Come along, it is home to me.

12

I said I would show you the inside of the Mendips, and so I will.'

Thus we went onward. We were now in the bowels of the Mendip hills – a range of limestone rocks stretching from the shores of the Bristol Channel into the middle of Somersetshire. Skeletons of great extinct beasts, and the remains of prehistoric men have been found thereabouts since that time; but at the date of which I write science was not so ardent as she is now, in the pursuit of the unknown; and we boys could only conjecture on subjects in which the boys of the present generation are well informed.

The dim sparkle of stalactites, which had continually appeared above us, now ranged lower and lower over our heads, till at last the walls of the cave seemed to bar further progress.

'There, this spot is what everybody calls the end of Nick's Pocket,' observed Steve, halting upon a mount of stalagmite, and throwing the beams of the candles around. 'But let me tell you,' he added, 'that here is a little arch, which I and some more boys found the other day. We did not go under it, but if you are agreed we will go in now and see how far we can get, for the fun of the thing. I brought these pieces of candle on purpose.' Steve looked what he felt – that there was a certain grandeur in a person like himself, to whom such mysteries as caves were mere playthings, because he had been born close alongside them. To do him justice, he was not altogether wrong, for he was a truly courageous fellow, and could look dangers in the face without flinching.

13

'I think we may as well leave fun out of the question,' I said, laughing; 'but we will go in.'

Accordingly he went forward, stooped, and entered the low archway, which, at first sight, appeared to be no more than a slight recess. I kept close at his heels. The arch gave access to a narrow tunnel or gallery, sloping downwards, and presently terminating in another cave, the floor of which spread out into a beautiful level of sand and shingle, interspersed with pieces of rock. Across the middle of this subterranean shore, as it might have been called, flowed a pellucid stream. Had my thoughts been in my books, I might have supposed we had descended to the nether regions, and had reached the Stygian shore; but it was out of sight, out of mind, with my classical studies then.

Beyond the stream, at some elevation, we could see a delightful recess in the crystallized stone work, like the apse of a Gothic church.

'How tantalizing!' exclaimed Steve, as he held the candles above his head, and peered across. 'If it were not for this trickling riband of water, we could get over and climb up into that arched nook, and sit there like kings on a crystal throne!'

'Perhaps it would not look so wonderful if we got close to it,' I suggested. 'But, for that matter, if you had a spade, you could soon turn the water out of the way, and into that hole.' The fact was, that just at that moment I had discovered a low opening on the left hand, like a human mouth, into which the stream would naturally flow, if a slight barrier of sand and pebbles were removed.

On looking there, also, Steve complimented me on the sharpness of my eyes. 'Yes,' he said, 'we could scrape away that bank, and the water would go straight into the hole surely enough. And we will. Let us go for a spade!'

I had not expected him to put the idea into practice; but it was no sooner said than done. We retraced our steps, and in a few minutes found ourselves again in the open air, where the sudden light overpowered our eyes for a while.

'Stay here, while I run home,' he said. 'I'll not be long.'

I agreed, and he disappeared. In a very short space he came back with the spade in his hand, and we again plunged in. This time the candles had been committed to my charge. When we had passed down the gallery into the second cave, Steve directed me to light a couple more of the candles, and stick them against a piece of rock, that he might have plenty of light to work by. This I did, and my stalwart cousin began to use the spade with a will, upon the breakwater of sand and stones.

The obstacle, which had been sufficient to turn the stream at a right angle, possibly for centuries, was of the most fragile description. Such instances of a slight obstruction diverting a sustained onset often occur in nature on a much larger scale. The Chesil Bank, for example, connecting the peninsula of Portland, in Dorsetshire, with the mainland, is a mere string of loose pebbles; yet it resists, by its shelving surface and easy curve, the mighty roll of the Channel seas, when urged upon the bank by the most furious south-west gales.

In a minute or two a portion of the purling stream discovered the opening Steve's spade was making in the sand, and began to flow through. The water assisted him in his remaining labours, supplementing every spadeful that he threw back, by washing aside ten. I remember that I was child enough, at the time, to clap my hands at the sight of larger and larger quantities of the brook tumbling in the form of a cascade down the dark chasm, where it had possibly never flowed before, or at any rate, never within the human period of the earth's history. In less than twenty minutes the whole stream trended off in this new direction, as calmly as if it had coursed there always. What had before been its bed now gradually drained dry, and we saw that we could walk across dryshod, with ease.

We speedily put the possibility into practice, and so reached the beautiful, glistening niche, that had tempted us to our engineering. We brought up into it the candles we had stuck against the rockwork farther down, placed them with the others around the niche, and prepared to rest awhile, the spot being quite dry.

'That's the way to overcome obstructions!' said Steve, triumphantly. 'I warrant nobody ever got so far as this before – at least, without wading up to his knees, in crossing that watercourse.'

My attention was so much attracted by the beautiful natural ornaments of the niche, that I hardly heeded his remark. These covered the greater part of the sides and roof; they were flesh-coloured, and assumed the form of pills, lace, coats of mail; in many places they quaintly

resembled the skin of geese after plucking, and in others the wattles of turkeys. All were decorated with water crystals.

'Well,' exclaimed I, 'I could stay here always!'

'So could I,' said Steve, 'if I had victuals enough. And some we'll have at once.'

Our bread and cheese and apples were unfolded, and we speedily devoured the whole. We then tried to chip pieces from the rock, and but indifferently succeeded, though while doing this we discovered some curious stones, like axe- and arrow-heads, at the bottom of the niche; but they had become partially attached to the floor by the limestone deposit, and could not be extracted.

'This is a long enough visit for today,' said my cousin, jumping up as one of the candles went out. 'We shall be left in the dark if we don't mind, and it would be no easy matter to find our way out without a light.'

Accordingly we gathered up the candles that remained, descended from the niche, re-crossed the deserted bed of the stream, and found our way to the open air, well pleased enough with the adventure, and promising each other to repeat it at an early date. On which account, instead of bringing away the unburnt candles, and the wood candlestick, and the spade, we laid these articles on a hidden shelf near the entrance, to be ready at hand at any time.

Having cleaned the tell-tale mud from our boots, we were on the point of entering the village, when our ears were attracted by a great commotion in the road below.

'What is it?' said I, standing still.

'Voices, I think,' replied Steve. 'Listen!'

It seemed to be a man in a violent frenzy. 'I think it is somebody out of his mind,' continued my cousin. 'I never heard a man rave so in my life.'

'Let us draw nearer,' said I.

We moved on, and soon came in sight of an individual, who, standing in the midst of the street, was gesticulating distractedly, and uttering invectives against something or other, to several villagers that had gathered around.

'Why, 'tis the miller!' said Steve. 'What can be the matter with him?'

We were not kept long in suspense, for we could soon hear his words distinctly. 'The money I've sunk here!' he was saying; 'the time – the honest labour – all for nothing! Only beggary afore me now! One month it was a new pair of mill-stones; then the back wall was cracked with the shaking, and had to be repaired; then I made a bad speculation in corn and dropped money that way! But 'tis nothing to this! My own freehold – the only staff and dependence o' my family – all useless now – all of us ruined!'

'Don't you take on so, Miller Griffin,' soothingly said one who proved to be the Man who had Failed. 'Take the ups and the downs, and maybe 'twill come right again.'

'Right again!' raved the miller; 'how can what's gone for ever come back again as 'twere afore – that's what I ask my wretched self – how can it?'

'We'll get up a subscription for ye,' said a local dairyman.

'I don't drink hard; I don't stay away from church, and I only grind into Sabbath hours when there's no getting through the work otherwise, and I pay my way like a man!'

'Yes – you do that,' corroborated the others.

'And yet, I be brought to ruinous despair, on this sixth day of September, Hannah Dominy; as if I were a villain! Oh, my mill, my mill-wheel – you'll never go round any more – never more!' The miller flung his arms upon the rail of the bridge, and buried his face in his hands.

'This raving is but making a bad job worse,' said the Man who had Failed. 'But who will listen to counsel on such matters?'

By this time we had drawn near, and Steve said, 'What's the cause of all this?'

'The river has dried up – all on a sudden,' said the dairyman, 'and so his mill won't go any more.'

I gazed instantly towards the stream, or rather what had been the stream. It was gone; and the mill-wheel, which had pattered so persistently when we entered the cavern, was silent. Steve and I instinctively stepped aside.

'The river gone dry!' Steve whispered.

'Yes,' said I. 'Why, Steve, don't you know why?'

My thoughts had instantly flown to our performance of turning the stream out of its channel in the cave, and I knew in a moment that this was the cause. Steve's silence showed me that he divined the same thing, and we stood gazing at each other in consternation.

CHAPTER
2

How we shone in
the eyes of the public

. . . on the green were several people seated at a table eating and drinking, and some younger members of the assembly dancing a reel in the background . . .

As soon as we had recovered ourselves we walked away, unconsciously approaching the river-bed, in whose hollows lay the dead and dying bodies of loach, sticklebacks, dace, and other small fry, which before our entrance into Nick's Pocket had raced merrily up and down the waterway. Farther on we perceived numbers of people ascending to the upper part of the village, with pitchers on their heads, and buckets yoked to their shoulders.

'Where are you going?' said Steve to one of those.

'To your mother's well for water,' was the answer. 'The river we have always been used to dip from is dried up. Oh, mercy me, what with the washing and cooking and brewing I don't know what we shall do to live, for 'tis killing work to bring water on your back so far!'

As may be supposed, all this gave me still greater

concern than before, and I hurriedly said to Steve that I was strongly of opinion that we ought to go back to the cave immediately, and turn the water into the old channel, seeing what harm we had unintentionally done by our manœuvre.

'Of course we'll go back – that's just what I was going to say,' returned Steve. 'We can set it all right again in half an hour, and the river will run the same as ever. Hullo – now you are frightened at what has happened! I can see you are.'

I told him that I was not exactly frightened, but that it seemed to me that we had caused a very serious catastrophe in the village, in driving the miller almost crazy, and killing the fish, and worrying the poor people into supposing they would never have enough water again for their daily use without fetching it from afar. 'Let us tell them how it came to pass,' I suggested, 'and then go and set it right.'

'Tell 'em – not I!' said Steve. 'We'll go back and put it right, and say nothing about it to anyone, and they will simply think it was caused by a temporary earthquake, or something of that sort.' He then broke into a vigorous whistle, and we retraced our steps together.

It occupied us but a few minutes to rekindle a light inside the cave, take out the spade from its nook, and penetrate to the scene of our morning exploit. Steve then fell to, and first rolling down a few large pieces of stone into the current, dexterously banked them up with clay from the other side of the cave, which caused the brook to swerve back into its original bed almost immediately.

'There,' said he, 'it is all just as it was when we first saw it – now let's be off.'

We did not dally long in the cavern; but when we gained the exterior we decided to wait there a little time till the villagers should have discovered the restoration of their stream, to watch the effect. Our waiting was but temporary; for in quick succession there burst upon our ears a shout, and then the starting of the mill-wheel patter.

At once we walked into the village street with an air of unconcern. The miller's face was creased with wrinkles of satisfaction; the countenances of the blacksmith, shoemaker, grocer, and dairyman were perceptibly brighter. These, and many others of West Poley, were gathered on the bridge over the mill-tail, and they were all holding a conversation with the parson of the parish, as to the strange occurrence.

Matters remained in a quiet state during the next two days. Then there was a remarkably fine and warm morning, and we proposed to cross the hills and descend into East Poley, the next village, which I had never seen. My aunt made no objection to the excursion, and we departed, ascending the hill in a straight line, without much regard to paths. When we had reached the summit, and were about half-way between the two villages, we sat down to recover breath. While we sat a man overtook us, and Steve recognized him as a neighbour.

'A bad job again for West Poley folks!' cried the man without halting.

'What's the matter now?' said Steve, and I started with curiosity.

'Oh, the river is dry again. It happened at a quarter past ten this morning, and it is thought it will never flow any more. The miller he's gone crazy, or all but so. And the washerwoman, she will have to be kept by the parish, because she can't get water to wash with; aye, 'tis a terrible time that's come. I'm off to try to hire a water-cart, but I fear I shan't hear of one.'

The speaker passed by, and on turning to Steve I found he was looking on the ground. 'I know how that's happened,' he presently said. 'We didn't make our embankment so strong as it was before, and so the water has washed it away.'

'Let's go back and mend it,' said I; and I proposed that we should reveal where the mischief lay, and get some of the labourers to build the bank up strong, that this might not happen again.

'No,' said Steve, 'since we are half-way we will have our day's pleasure. It won't hurt the West Poley people to be out of water for one day. We'll return home a little earlier then we intended, and put it all in order again, either ourselves, or by the help of some men.'

Having gone about a mile and a half farther we reached the brow of the descent into East Poley, the place we had come to visit. Here we beheld advancing towards us a stranger whose actions we could not at first interpret. But as the distance between us and him lessened we discerned, to our surprise, that he was in convulsions of laughter. He would laugh until he was tired, then he would stand still gazing on the ground, as if quite pre-occupied, then he would burst out laughing again and walk on. No sooner did he see us two boys than he placed his hat upon his walking-stick, twirled it and cried 'Hurrah!'

I was so amused that I could not help laughing with him; and when he came abreast of us Steve said, 'Good morning; may I ask what it is that makes you laugh so?'

But the man was either too self-absorbed or too super-cilious to vouchsafe to us any lucid explanation. 'What makes me laugh?' he said. 'Why, good luck, my boys! Perhaps when you are as lucky, you will laugh too.' Saying which he walked on and left us; and we could hear him exclaiming to himself, 'Well done – hurrah!' as he sank behind the ridge.

Without pausing longer we descended towards the village, and soon reached its outlying homesteads. Our path intersected a green field dotted with trees, on the other side of which was an inn. As we drew near we heard the strains of a fiddle, and presently perceived a fiddler standing on a chair outside the inn door; whilst on the green in front were several people seated at a table eating and drinking, and some younger members of the assembly dancing a reel in the background.

We naturally felt much curiosity as to the cause of the merriment, which we mentally connected with that of the man we had met just before. Turning to one of the old men feasting at the table, I said to him as civilly as I could, 'Why are you all so lively in this parish, sir?'

'Because we are in luck's way just now, for we don't get a new river every day. Hurrah!'

'A new river?' said Steve and I in one breath.

'Yes,' said one of our interlocutors, waving over the table a ham-bone he had been polishing. 'Yesterday afternoon a river of beautiful water burst out of the quarry at the higher end of this bottom; in an hour or so it stopped again. This morning, about a quarter past ten, it burst out again, and it is running now as if it would run always.'

'It will make all land and houses in this parish worth double as much as afore,' said another; 'for want of water is the one thing that has always troubled us, forcing us to sink deep wells, and even then being hard put to, to get enough for our cattle. Now, we have got a river, and the place will grow to a town.'

'It is as good as two hundred pounds to me!' said one who looked like a grazier.

'And two hundred and fifty to me!' cried another, who seemed to be a brewer.

'And sixty pound a year to me, and to every man here in the building trade!' said a third.

As soon as we could withdraw from the company, our thoughts found vent in words.

'I ought to have seen it!' said Steve. 'Of course if you stop a stream from flowing in one direction, it must force its way out in another.'

'I wonder where their new stream is,' said I.

We looked round. After some examination we saw a depression in the centre of a pasture, and, approaching it, beheld the stream meandering along over the grass, the current not having had as yet sufficient time to scour a bed. Walking down to the brink, we were lost in wonder at what we had unwittingly done, and quite bewildered at the strange events we had caused. Feeling, now, that we had walked far enough from home for one day, we turned, and, in a brief time, entered a road pointed out by Steve, as one that would take us to West Poley by a shorter cut than our outward route.

As we ascended the hill, Steve looked round at me. I suppose my face revealed my thoughts, for he said, 'You are amazed, Leonard, at the wonders we have accomplished without knowing it. To tell the truth, so am I.'

I said that what staggered me was this – that we could not turn back the water into its old bed now, without doing as much harm to the people of East Poley by taking it away, as we should do good to the people of West Poley by restoring it.

'True,' said Steve, 'that's what bothers me. Though I think we have done more good to these people than we have done harm to the others, and I think these are rather nicer people than those in our village, don't you?'

I objected that even if this were so, we could have no right to take water away from one set of villagers and give it to another set without consulting them.

Steve seemed to feel the force of the argument; but as his mother had a well of her own he was less inclined to side with his native place than he might have been if his own household had been deprived of water, for the benefit of the East Poleyites. The matter was still in suspense, when, weary with our day's pilgrimage, we reached the mill.

The mill-pond was drained to its bed; the wheel stood motionless; yet a noise came from the interior. It was not the noise of machinery, but of the nature of blows, followed by bitter expostulations. On looking in, we were grieved to see that the miller, in a great rage, was holding his apprentice by the collar, and beating him with a strap.

The miller was a heavy, powerful man, and more than a match for his apprentice and us two boys besides; but Steve reddened with indignation, and asked the miller, with some spirit, why he served the poor fellow so badly.

'He says he'll leave,' stormed the frantic miller. 'What right hev he to say he'll leave, I should like to know!'

'There is no work for me to do, now the mill won't go,' said the apprentice, meekly; 'and the agreement was that I should be at liberty to leave if work failed in the mill. He keeps me here and don't pay me; and I be at my wits' end how to live.'

'Just shut up!' said the miller. 'Go and work in the garden! Mill-work or no mill-work, you'll stay on.'

Job, as the miller's boy was called, had won the good-will of Steve, and Steve was now ardent to do him a good turn. Looking over the bridge, we saw, passing by, the Man who had Failed. He was considered an authority on such matters as these, and we begged him to come in. In a few minutes the miller was set down, and it was proved to him that, by the terms of Job's indentures, he was no longer bound to remain.

'I have to thank you for this,' said the miller, savagely, to Steve. 'Ruined in every way! I may as well die!'

But my cousin cared little for the miller's opinion, and we came away, thanking the Man who had Failed for his interference, and receiving the warmest expressions of gratitude from poor Job; who, it appeared, had suffered much ill-treatment from his irascible master, and was overjoyed to escape to some other employment.

We went to bed early that night, on account of our long walk; but we were far too excited to sleep at once. It was scarcely dark as yet, and the nights being still warm the window was left open as it had been left during the summer. Thus we could hear everything that passed without. People were continually coming to dip water from my aunt's well; they gathered round it in groups, and discussed the remarkable event which had latterly occurred for the first time in parish history.

'My belief is that witchcraft have done it,' said the shoemaker, 'and the only remedy that I can think o', is for one of us to cut across to Bartholomew Gann, the white wizard, and get him to tell us how to counteract it. 'Tis a long pull to his house for a little man, such as I be, but I'll walk it if nobody else will.'

'Well, there's no harm in your going,' said another. 'We can manage by drawing from Mrs Draycot's well for for a few days; but something must be done, or the miller'll be ruined, and the washerwoman can't hold out long.'

When these personages had drawn water and retired, Steve spoke across from his bed to me in mine. 'We've

done more good than harm, that I'll maintain. The miller is the only man seriously upset, and he's not a man to deserve consideration. It has been the means of freeing poor Job, which is another good thing. Then, the people in East Poley that we've made happy are two hundred and fifty, and there are only a hundred in this parish, even if all of 'em are made miserable.'

I returned some reply, though the state of affairs

was, in truth, one rather suited to the genius of Jeremy Bentham than to me. But the problem in utilitarian philosophy was shelved by Steve exclaiming, 'I have it! I see how to get some real glory out of this!'

I demanded how, with much curiosity.

'You'll swear not to tell anybody, or let it be known anyhow that we are at the bottom of it all?'

I am sorry to say that my weak compunctions gave way under stress of this temptation; and I solemnly declared that I would reveal nothing, unless he agreed with me that it would be best to do so. Steve made me swear, in the tone of Hamlet to the Ghost, and when I had done this, he sat up in his bed to announce his scheme.

'First, we'll go to Job,' said Steve. 'Take him into the secret; show him the cave; give him a spade and pickaxe; and tell him to turn off the water from East Poley at, say, twelve o'clock, for a little while. Then we'll go to the East Poley boys and declare ourselves to be magicians.'

'Magicians?' I said.

'Magicians, able to dry up rivers, or to make 'em run at will,' he repeated.

'I see it!' I almost screamed, in my delight.

'To show our power, we'll name an hour for drying up theirs, and making it run again after a short time. Of course, we'll say the hour we've told Job to turn the water in the cave. Won't they think something of us then?'

I was enchanted. The question of mischief or not mischief was as indifferent to me now as it was to Steve – for which indifference we got rich deserts, as will be seen in the sequel.

'And to look grand and magical,' continued he, 'we'll get some gold lace that I know of in the garret, on an old coat my grandfather wore in the Yeomanry Cavalry, and put it round our caps, and make ourselves great beards with horse-hair. They will look just like real ones at a little distance off.'

'And we must each have a wand!' said I, explaining that I knew how to make excellent wands, white as snow, by peeling a couple of straight willows; and that I could do all that in the morning while he was preparing the beards.

Thus we discussed and settled the matter, and at length fell asleep – to dream of tomorrow's triumphs among the boys of East Poley, till the sun of that morrow shone in upon our faces and woke us. We arose promptly and made our preparations, having *carte blanche* from my Aunt Draycot to spend the days of my visit as we chose.

Our first object on leaving the farmhouse was to find Job Tray, apprise him of what it was necessary that he should know, and induce him to act as confederate. We found him outside the garden of his lodging; he told us he had nothing to do till the following Monday, when a farmer had agreed to hire him. On learning the secret of the river-head, and what we proposed to do, he expressed his glee by a low laugh of amazed delight, and readily promised to assist as bidden. It took us some little time to show him the inner cave, the tools, and to arrange candles for him, so that he might enter without difficulty just after eleven and do the trick. When this was all settled we put Steve's watch on a ledge in the cave, that Job might know the exact time, and came out to ascend the hills that divided the eastern from the western village.

For obvious reasons we did not appear in magician's guise till we had left the western vale some way behind us. Seated on the limestone ridge, removed from all observation, we set to work at preparing ourselves. I peeled the two willows we had brought with us to be used as magic wands, and Steve pinned the pieces of old lace round our caps, congratulating himself on the fact of the lace not being new, which would thus convey the impression that we had exercised the wizard's calling for some years. Our last adornments were the beards; and, finally equipped, we descended on the other side.

Our plan was now to avoid the upper part of East Poley, which we had traversed on the preceding day, and to strike into the parish at a point farther down, where the humble cottages stood, and where we were both absolutely unknown. An hour's additional walking brought us to this spot, which, as the crow flies, was not more than half so far from West Poley as the road made it.

The first boys we saw were some playing in an orchard near the new stream, which novelty had evidently been the attraction that had brought them there. It was an opportunity for opening the campaign, especially as the hour was long after eleven, and the cessation of water consequent on Job's performance at a quarter past might be expected to take place as near as possible to twelve, allowing the five and forty minutes from eleven-fifteen, as the probable time that would be occupied by the stream in travelling to the point we had reached.

I forget at this long distance of years the exact words used by Steve in addressing the strangers; but to the best of my recollection they were, 'How d'ye do, gentlemen, and how does the world use ye?' I distinctly remember the sublimity he threw into his gait, and how slavishly I imitated him in the same.

The boys made some indifferent answer, and Steve continued, 'You will kindly present us with some of those apples, I presume, considering what we are?'

They regarded us dubiously, and at last one of them said, 'What are you, that you should expect apples from us?'

'We are travelling magicians,' replied Steve. 'You may have heard of us, for by our power this new river has begun to flow. Rhombustas is my name, and this is my familiar, Balcazar.'

'I don't believe it,' said an incredulous one from behind.

'Very well, gentlemen; we can't help that. But if you give us some apples we'll prove our right to the title.'

'Be hanged if we will give you any apples,' said the boy who held the basket; 'since it is already proved that magicians are impossible.'

'In that case,' said Steve, 'we – we –'

'Will perform just the same,' interrupted I, for I feared Steve had forgotten that the time was at hand when the stream would be interrupted by Job, whether he willed it or not.

'We will stop the water of your new river at twelve o'clock this day, when the sun crosses the meridian,' said Rhombustas, 'as a punishment for your want of generosity.'

'Do it!' said the boys incredulously.

'Come here, Balcazar,' said Steve. We walked together to the edge of the stream; then we muttered, *Hi, hae, haec, horum, harum, horum*, and stood waving our wands.

'The river do run just the same,' said the strangers derisively.

'The spell takes time to work,' said Rhombustas, adding in an aside to me, 'I hope that fellow Job has not forgotten, or we shall be hooted out of the place.'

There we stood, waving and waving our white sticks, hoping and hoping that we should succeed; while still the river flowed. Seven or ten minutes passed thus; and then, when we were nearly broken down by ridicule, the stream diminished its volume. All eyes were instantly bent on the water, which sank so low as to be in a short time but a narrow rivulet. The faithful Job had performed his task. By the time that the clock of the church tower struck twelve the river was almost dry.

The boys looked at each other in amazement, and at us with awe. They were too greatly concerned to speak except in murmurs to each other.

'You see the result of your conduct, unbelieving strangers,' said Steve, drawing boldly up to them. 'And I seriously ask that you hand over those apples before we bring further troubles upon you and your village. We give you five minutes to consider.'

'We decide at once!' cried the boys. 'The apples be yours and welcome.'

'Thank you, gentlemen,' said Steve, while I added, 'For your readiness the river shall run again in two or three minutes' time.'

'Oh – ah, yes,' said Steve, adding heartily in under-tones, 'I had forgotten that!'

Almost as soon as the words were spoken we per-ceived a little increase in the mere dribble of water which now flowed, whereupon he waved his wand and mur-mured more words. The liquid thread swelled and rose; and in a few minutes was the same as before. Our triumph was complete; and the suspension had been so temporary that probably nobody in the village had noticed it but ourselves and the boys.

CHAPTER
3

How we were caught
in our own trap

*. . . 'Indeed, sir, you need not ruin my premises so!' she
said with tears in her eyes . . .*

At this acme of our glory who should come past but a
hedger whom Steve recognized as an inhabitant of West
Poley; unluckily for our greatness the hedger also recognized Steve.

'Well, Maister Stevey, what be you doing over in these
parts then? And yer little cousin, too, upon my word!
And beards – why ye've made yerselves ornamental!
haw, haw!'

In great trepidation Steve moved on with the man,
endeavouring, thus, to get him out of hearing of the
boys.

'Look here,' said Steve to me on leaving that outspoken
rustic; 'I think this is enough for one day. We'd better go
farther before they guess all.'

'With all my heart,' said I. And we walked on.

'But what's going on here?' said Steve, when, turning a

corner of the hedge, we perceived an altercation in progress hard by. The parties proved to be a poor widow and a corn-factor, who had been planning a water-wheel lower down the stream. The latter had dammed the water for his purpose to such an extent as to submerge the poor woman's garden, turning it into a lake.

'Indeed, sir, you need not ruin my premises so!' she said with tears in her eyes. 'The mill-pond can be kept from overflowing my garden by a little banking and digging; it will be just as well for your purpose to keep it lower down, as to let it spread out into a great pool here. The house and garden are yours by law, sir; that's true.

But my father built the house, and, oh, sir, I was born here, and I should like to end my days under its roof!'

'Can't help it, mis'ess,' said the corn-factor. 'Your garden is a mill-pond already made, and to get a hollow farther down I should have to dig at great expense. There is a very nice cottage up the hill, where you can live as well as here. When your father died the house came into my hands; and I can do what I like with my own.'

The woman went sadly away indoors. As for Steve and myself, we were deeply moved, as we looked at the pitiable sight of the poor woman's garden, the tops of the gooseberry bushes forming small islands in the water, and her few apple-trees standing immersed half-way up their stems.

'The man is a rascal,' said Steve. 'I perceive that it is next to impossible, in this world, to do good to one set of folks without doing harm to another.'

'Since we have not done all good to these people of East Poley,' said I, 'there is a reason for restoring the river to its old course through West Poley.'

'But then,' said Steve, 'if we turn back the stream, we shall be starting Miller Griffin's mill; and then, by the terms of his 'prenticeship, poor Job will have to go back to him and be beaten again! It takes good brains no less than a good heart to do what's right towards all.'

Quite unable to solve the problem into which we had drifted, we retraced our steps, till, at a stile, within half a mile of West Poley, we beheld Job awaiting us.

'Well, how did it act?' he asked with great eagerness. 'Just as the hands of your watch got to a quarter past eleven, I began to shovel away, and turned the water in no time. But I didn't turn it where you expected – not I – 'twould have started the mill for a few minutes, and I wasn't going to do that.'

'Then where did you turn it?' cried Steve.

'I found another hole,' said Job.

'A third one?'

'Ay, hee, hee! a third one! So I pulled the stones aside from this new hole, and shovelled the clay, and down the water went with a gush. When it had run down there a few minutes, I turned it back to the East Poley hole, as you ordered me to do. But as to getting it back to the old West Poley hole, that I'd never do.'

Steve then explained that we no more wished the East village to have the river than the West village, on account

of our discovery that equal persecution was going on in the one place as in the other. Job's news of a third channel solved our difficulty. 'So we'll go at once and send it down this third channel,' concluded he.

We walked back to the village, and, as it was getting late, and we were tired, we decided to do nothing that night, but told Job to meet us in the cave on the following evening, to complete our work there.

All next day my cousin was away from home, at market for his mother, and he had arranged with me that if he did not return soon enough to join me before going to Nick's Pocket, I should proceed thither, where he would meet me on his way back from the market-town. The day passed anxiously enough for me, for I had some doubts of a very grave kind as to our right to deprive two parishes of water on our own judgement, even though that should be, as it was, honestly based on our aversion to tyranny. However, dusk came on at last, and Steve not appearing from market, I concluded that I was to meet him at the cave's mouth.

To this end I strolled out in that direction, and there being as yet no hurry, I allowed myself to be tempted out of my path by a young rabbit, which, however, I failed to capture. This divergence had brought me inside a field, behind a hedge, and before I could resume my walk along the main road, I heard some persons passing along the other side. The words of their conversation arrested me in a moment.

''Tis a strange story if it's true,' came through the hedge in the tones of Miller Griffin. 'We know that East

Poley folk will say queer things; but the boys wouldn't say that it was the work of magicians if they hadn't some ground for it.'

'And how do they explain it?' asked the shoemaker.

'They say that these two young fellows passed down their lane about twelve o'clock, dressed like magicians, and offered to show their power by stopping the river. The East Poley boys challenged 'em; when, by George, they did stop the river! They said a few words, and it dried up like magic. Now mark my words, my suspicion is this: these two gamesters have somehow got at the river-head, and been tampering with it in some way. The water that runs down East Poley bottom is the water that ought, by rights, to be running through my mill.'

'A very pretty piece of mischief, if that's the case!' said the shoemaker. 'I've never liked them lads, particularly that Steve – for not a boot or shoe hev he had o' me since he's been old enough to choose for himself – not a pair, or even a mending. But I don't see how they could do all this, even if they had got at the river-head. 'Tis a spring out of the hill, isn't it? And how could they stop the spring?'

It seemed that the miller could offer no explanation, for no answer was returned. My course was clear: to join Job and Steve at Nick's Pocket immediately; tell them that we were suspected, and to get them to give over further proceeding, till we had stated our difficulties to some person of experience – say the Man who had Failed.

I accordingly ran like a hare over the clover inside the

hedge, and soon was far away from the interlocutors. Drawing near the cave, I was relieved to see Steve's head against the sky. I joined him at once, and recounted to him, in haste, what had passed.

He meditated. 'They don't even now suspect that the secret lies in the cavern,' said he.

'But they will soon,' said I.

'Well, perhaps they may,' he answered. 'But there will be time for us to finish our undertaking, and turn the stream down the third hole. When we've done that we can consider which of the villages is most worthy to have the river, and act accordingly.'

'Do let us take a good wise man into our confidence,' I said.

After a little demurring, he agreed that as soon as we had completed the scheme we would state the case to a competent adviser, and let it be settled fairly. 'And now,' he said, 'where's Job? Inside the cave, no doubt, as it is past the time I promised to be here.'

Stepping inside the cave's mouth, we found that the candles and other things which had been deposited there were removed. The probability being that Job had arrived and taken them in with him, we groped our way along in the dark, helped by an occasional match which Steve struck from a box he carried. Descending the gallery at the farther end of the outer cavern, we discerned a glimmer at the remote extremity, and soon beheld Job working with all his might by the light of one of the candles.

'I've almost got it to the hole that leads to neither of the

Poleys, but I wouldn't actually turn it till you came,' he said, wiping his face.

We told him that the neighbours were on our track, and might soon guess that we performed our tricks in Nick's Pocket, and come there, and find that the stream flowed through the cave before rising in the spring at the top of the village; and asked him to turn the water at once, and be off with us.

'Ah!' said Job, mournfully, 'then 'tis over with me! They will be here tomorrow, and will turn back the stream, and the mill will go again, and I shall have to finish my time as 'prentice to the man who did this!' He pulled up his shirt sleeve, and showed us on his arm several stripes and bruises – black and blue and green – the tell-tale relics of old blows from the miller.

Steve reddened with indignation. 'I would give anything to stop up the channels to the two Poleys so close that they couldn't be found again!' he said. 'Couldn't we do it with stones and clay? Then, if they come here 'twould make no difference, and the water would flow down the third hole for ever, and we should save Job and the widow after all.'

'We can but try it,' said Job, willing to fall in with anything that would hinder his recall to the mill. 'Let's set to work.'

Steve took the spade, and Job the pickaxe. First they finished what Job had begun – the turning of the stream into the third tunnel or crevice, which led to neither of the Poleys. This done, they set to work jamming stones into the other two openings, treading earth and clay around

them, and smoothing over the whole in such a manner that nobody should notice they had ever existed. So intent were we on completing it that – to our utter disaster – we did not notice what was going on behind us.

I was the first to look round, and I well remember why. My ears had been attracted by a slight change of tone in the purl of the water down the new crevice discovered by Job, and I was curious to learn the reason of it. The sight that met my gaze might well have appalled a stouter and older heart than mine. Instead of pouring down out of sight, as it had been doing when we last looked, the stream was choked by a rising pool into which it boiled, showing at a glance that what we had innocently believed to be another outlet for the stream was only a blind passage or cul-de-sac, which the water, when first turned that way by Job, had not been left long enough to fill before it was turned back again.

'Oh, Steve – Job!' I cried, and could say no more.

They gazed round at once, and saw the situation. Nick's Pocket had become a cauldron. The surface of the rising pool stood, already, far above the mouth of the gallery by which we had entered, and which was our only way out – stood far above the old exit of the stream to West Poley, now sealed up; far above the second outlet to East Poley, discovered by Steve, and also sealed up by our fatal ingenuity. We had been spending the evening in making a closed bottle of the cave, in which the water was now rising to drown us.

'There is one chance for us – only one,' said Steve in a dry voice.

'What one?' we asked in a breath.

'To open the old channel leading to the mill,' said Steve.

'I would almost as soon be drowned as do that,' murmured Job gloomily. 'But there's more lives than my own, so I'll work with a will. Yet how be we to open any channel at all?'

The question was, indeed, of awful aptness. It was extremely improbable that we should have power to reopen either conduit now. Both those exits had been funnel-shaped cavities, narrowing down to mere fissures at the bottom; and the stones and earth we had hurled into these cavities had wedged themselves together by their own weight. Moreover – and here was the rub – it might have been possible to pull the stones out while they remained unsubmerged, but the whole mass was now under water, which enlarged the task of reopening the channel to Herculean dimensions.

But we did not know my cousin Steve as yet. 'You will help me here,' he said authoritatively to Job, pointing to the West Poley conduit. 'Lenny, my poor cousin,' he went on, turning to me, 'we are in a bad way. All you can do is to stand in the niche, and make the most of the candles by keeping them from the draught with your hat, and burning only one at a time. How many have we, Job?'

'Ten ends, some long, some short,' said Job.

'They will burn many hours,' said Steve. 'And now we must dive, and begin to get out the stones.'

They had soon stripped off all but their drawers, and, laying their clothes on the dry floor of the niche behind me, stepped down into the middle of the cave. The water here was already above their waists, and at the original gulley-hole leading to West Poley spring was proportionately deeper. Into this part, nevertheless, Steve dived. I have recalled his appearance a hundred – aye, a thousand times since that day, as he came up – his crown bobbing into the dim candlelight like a floating apple. He stood upright, bearing in his arms a stone as big as his head.

'That's one of 'em!' he said as soon as he could speak. 'But there are many, many more!'

He threw the stone behind; while Job, wasting no time, had already dived in at the same point. Job was not such a good diver as Steve, in the sense of getting easily at the bottom; but he could hold his breath longer, and it was an extraordinary length of time before his head emerged above the surface, though his feet were kicking in the air more than once. Clutched to his chest, when he rose, was a second large stone, and a couple of small ones with it. He threw the whole to a distance; and Steve, having now recovered breath, plunged again into the hole.

But I can hardly bear to recall this terrible hour even now, at a distance of many years. My suspense was, perhaps, more trying than that of the others, for, unlike them, I could not escape reflection by superhuman physical efforts. My task of economizing the candles, by shading them with my hat, was not to be compared, in difficulty, to theirs; but I would gladly have changed places, if it had been possible to such a small boy, with

Steve and Job, so intolerable was it to remain motionless in the desperate circumstances.

Thus I watched the rising of the waters, inch by inch, and on that account was in a better position than they to draw an inference as to the probable end of the adventure.

There were a dozen, or perhaps twenty, stones to extract before we could hope for an escape of the pent mass of water; and the difficulty of extracting them increased with each successive attempt, in two ways, by the greater actual remoteness of stone after stone, and by its greater relative remoteness through the rising of the pool. However, the sustained, gallant struggles of my two comrades succeeded, at last, in raising the number of stones extracted to seven. Then we fancied that some slight passage had been obtained for the stream; for, though the terrible pool still rose higher, it seemed to rise less rapidly.

After several attempts, in which Steve and Job brought up nothing, there came a declaration from them that they could do no more. The lower stones were so tightly jammed between the sides of the fissure that no human strength seemed able to pull them out.

Job and Steve both came up from the water. They were exhausted and shivering, and well they might be. 'We must try some other way,' said Steve.

'What way?' asked I.

Steve looked at me. 'You are a very good little fellow to stand this so well!' he said, with something like tears in his eyes.

They soon got on their clothes; and, having given up all hope of escape downward, we turned our eyes to the roof of the cave, on the chance of discovering some outlet there.

There was not enough light from our solitary candle to show us all the features of the vault in detail; but we could see enough to gather that it formed anything but a perfect dome. The roof was rather a series of rifts and projections, and high on one side, almost lost in the shades, there was a larger and deeper rift than elsewhere, forming a sort of loft, the back parts of which were invisible, extending we knew not how far. It was through this overhanging rift that the draught seemed to come which had caused our candle to gutter and flare.

To think of reaching an opening so far above our heads, so advanced into the ceiling of the cave as to require a fly's power of walking upside down to approach it, was mere waste of time. We bent our gaze elsewhere. On the same side with the niche in which we stood there was a small narrow ledge quite near at hand, and to gain it my two stalwart companions now exerted all their strength.

By cutting a sort of step with the pickaxe, Job was enabled to obtain a footing about three feet above the level of our present floor, and then he called to me.

'Now, Leonard, you be the lightest. Do you hop up here, and climb upon my shoulder, and then I think you will be tall enough to scramble to the ledge, so as to help us up after you.'

I leapt up beside him, clambered upon his stout back as he bade me, and, springing from his shoulder, reached the ledge. He then handed up the pickaxe, directed me how to make its point firm into one of the crevices on the top of the ledge; next, to lie down, hold on to the handle of the pickaxe and give him my other hand. I obediently acted, when he sprang up, and turning, assisted Steve to do likewise.

We had now reached the highest possible coign of vantage left to us, and there remained nothing more to do but wait and hope that the encroaching water would find some unseen outlet before reaching our level.

Job and Steve were so weary from their exertions that

they seemed almost indifferent as to what happened, provided they might only be allowed to rest. However, they tried to devise new schemes, and looked wistfully over the surface of the pool.

'I wonder if it rises still?' I said. 'Perhaps not, after all.'

'Then we shall only exchange drowning for starving,' said Steve.

Job, instead of speaking, had endeavoured to answer my query by stopping down and stretching over the ledge with his arm. His face was very calm as he rose again. 'It will be drowning,' he said almost inaudibly, and held up his hand, which was wet.

4

How older heads than ours became concerned

. . . . the miller was unable to check himself, and fell over headlong into the whirling pool beneath . . .

THE water had risen so high that Job could touch its surface from our retreat.

We now, in spite of Job's remark, indulged in the dream that, provided the water would stop rising, we might, in the course of time, find a way out somehow, and Job by-and-by said, 'Perhaps round there in the dark may be places where we could crawl out, if we could only see them well enough to swim across to them. Couldn't we send a candle round that way?'

'How?' said I and Steve.

'By a plan I have thought of,' said he. Taking off his hat, which was of straw, he cut with his pocket-knife a little hole in the middle of the crown. Into this he stuck a piece of candle, lighted it, and lying down to reach the surface of the water as before, lowered the hat till it rested afloat.

There was, as Job had suspected, a slight circular current in the apparently still water, and the hat moved on slowly. Our six eyes became riveted on the voyaging candle as if it were a thing of fascination. It travelled away from us, lighting up in its progress unsuspected protuberances and hollows, but revealing to our eager stare no spot of safety or of egress. It went farther and yet farther into darkness, till it became like a star alone in a sky. Then it crossed from left to right. Then it gradually turned and enlarged, was lost behind jutting crags, reappeared, and journeyed back towards us, till it again floated under the ledge on which we stood, and we gathered it in. It had made a complete circuit of the cavern, the circular motion of the water being caused by the inpour of the spring, and it had showed us no means of escape at all.

Steve spoke, saying solemnly, 'This is all my fault!'

'No,' said Job. 'For you would not have tried to stop the mill-stream if it had not been to save me.'

'But I began it all,' said Steve, bitterly. 'I see now the foolishness of presumption. What right had I to take upon myself the ordering of a stream of water that scores of men three times my age get their living by?'

'I thought overmuch of myself, too,' said Job. 'It was hardly right to stop the grinding of flour that made bread for a whole parish, for my poor sake. We ought to ha' got the advice of some one wi' more experience than ourselves.'

We then stood silent. The impossibility of doing more pressed in upon our senses like a chill, and I suggested that we should say our prayers.

'I think we ought,' said Steve, and Job assenting, we all three knelt down. After this a sad sense of resignation fell on us all, and there being now no hopeful attempt which they could make for deliverance, the sleep that excitement had hitherto withstood overcame both Steve and Job. They leant back and were soon unconscious.

Not having exerted myself to the extent they had done, I felt no sleepiness whatever. So I sat beside them with my eyes wide open, holding and protecting the candle mechanically, and wondering if it could really be possible that we were doomed to die.

I do not know how or why, but there came into my mind during this suspense the words I had read somewhere at school, as being those of Flaminius, the consul, when he was penned up at Thrasymene: 'Friends, we must not hope to get out of this by vows and prayers alone. 'Tis by fortitude and strength we must escape.' The futility of any such resolve in my case was apparent enough, and yet the words were sufficient to lead me to scan the roof of the cave once more.

When the opening up there met my eye I said to myself, 'I wonder where that hole leads to?' Picking up a stone about the size of my fist I threw it with indifference, though with a good aim, towards the spot. The stone passed through the gaping orifice, and I heard it alight within like a tennis ball.

But its noise did not cease with its impact. The fall was succeeded by a helter-skelter kind of rattle which, though it receded in the distance, I could hear for a long time with distinctness, owing, I suppose, to the reflection or echo from the top and sides of the cave. It denoted that on the other side of that dark mouth yawning above me there was a slope downward – possibly into another cave, and that the stone had ricocheted down the incline. 'I wonder where it leads?' I murmured again aloud.

Something greeted my ears at that moment of my pronouncing the words 'where it leads' that caused me wellnigh to leap out of my shoes. Even now I cannot think of it without experiencing a thrill. It came from the gaping hole.

If my readers can imagine for themselves the sensations of a timid bird, who, while watching the approach of his captors to strangle him, feels his wings loosening from the tenacious snare, and flight again possible, they may conceive my emotions when I realized that what greeted my ears from above were the words of a human tongue, direct from the cavity.

'Where, in the name of fortune, did that stone come from?'

The voice was the voice of the miller.

'Be dazed if I know – but 'a nearly broke my head!' The reply was that of the shoemaker.

'Steve – Job!' said I. They awoke with a start and exclamation. I tried to shout, but could not. 'They have found us – up there – the miller – shoemaker!' I whispered, pointing to the hole aloft.

Steve and Job understood. Perhaps the sole ingredient in this sudden revival of our hopes, which could save us from fainting with joy, was the one actually present – that our discoverer was the adversary whom we had been working to circumvent. But such antagonism as his weighed little in the scale with our present despairing circumstances.

We all three combined our voices in one shout – a shout which roused echoes in the cavern that probably had never been awakened since the upheaval of the Mendips, in whose heart we stood. When the shout died away we listened with parted lips.

Then we heard the miller speak again. 'Faith, and believe me – 'tis the rascals themselves! A-throwing stones – a-trying to terrify us off the premises! Did man ever know the like impudence? We have found the clue to the water mystery at last – may be at their pranks at this very moment! Clamber up here; and if I don't put about their backs the greenest stick that ever growed, I'm no grinder o' corn!'

Then we heard a creeping movement from the orifice over our heads, as of persons on their hands and knees; a puffing, as of fat men out of breath; sudden interjections, such as can be found in a list in any boy's grammar-book, and, therefore, need not be repeated here. All this was followed by a faint glimmer, about equal to that from our own candle, bursting from the gap on high, and the cautious appearance of a head over the ledge.

It was the visage of the shoemaker. Beside it rose another in haste, exclaiming, 'Urrr – r! The rascals!' and waving a stick. Almost before we had recognized this as the miller, he, climbing forward with too great impetuosity, and not perceiving that the edge of the orifice was so near, was unable to check himself. He fell over headlong, and was precipitated a distance of some thirty feet into the whirling pool beneath.

Job's face, which, until this catastrophe, had been quite white and rigid at the sight of his old enemy, instantly put on a more humane expression. 'We mustn't let him drown,' he said. 'No,' said Steve, 'but how can we save him in such an awkward place?'

There was, for the moment, however, no great cause for anxiety. The miller was a stout man, and could swim, though but badly – his power to keep afloat being due rather to the adipose tissues which composed his person, than to skill. But his immersion had been deep, and when

he rose to the surface he was bubbling and spluttering wildly.

'Hu, hu, hu, hu! O, ho – I am drownded!' he gasped. 'I am a dead man and miller – all on account of those villainous – I mean good boys! – If Job would only help me out I would give him such a dressing – blessing! I would say – as he never felt the force of before. Oh, bub, bub, hu, hu, hu!'

Job had listened to this with attention. 'Now, will you let me rule in this matter?' he said to Steve.

'With all my heart,' said Steve.

'Look here, Miller Griffin,' then said Job, speaking over the pool, 'you can't expect me or my comrades to help ye until you treat us civilly. No mixed words o' that sort will we stand. Fair and square, or not at all. You must give us straightforward assurance that you will do us no harm; and that if the water runs in your stream again, and the mill goes, and I finish out my 'prenticeship, you treat me

63

well. If you won't promise this, you are a dead man in that water tonight.'

'A master has a right over his 'prentice, body and soul!' cried the miller, desperately, as he swam round, 'and I have a right over you – and I won't be drownded!'

'I fancy you will,' said Job, quietly. 'Your friends be too high above to get at ye.'

'What must I promise ye, then, Job – hu – hu – hu – bub, bub, bub!'

'Say, if I ever strike Job Tray again, he shall be at liberty to leave my service forthwith, and go to some other employ, and this is the solemn oath of me, Miller Griffin. Say that in the presence of these witnesses.'

'Very well – I say it – bub, bub – I say it.' And the miller repeated the words.

'Now, I'll help ye out,' said Job. Lying down on his stomach, he held out the handle of the shovel to the floating miller, and hauled him towards the ledge on which we stood. Then Steve took one of the miller's hands, and Job the other, and he mounted up beside us.

'Saved – saved!' cried Miller Griffin.

'You must stand close in,' said Steve, 'for there isn't much room on this narrow shelf.'

'Ay, yes I will,' replied the saved man gladly. 'And now, let's get out of this dark place as soon as we can – Ho! – Cobbler Jones! here we be coming up to ye – but I don't see him!'

'Nor I,' said Steve. 'Where is he?'

The whole four of us stared with all our vision at the

opening the miller had fallen from. But his companion had vanished.

'Well – never mind,' said Miller Griffin, genially; 'we'll follow. Which is the way?'

'There's no way – we can't follow,' answered Steve.

'Can't follow!' echoed the miller, staring round, and perceiving for the first time that the ledge was a prison. 'What – *not saved*!' he shrieked. 'Not able to get out from here?'

'We be not saved unless your friend comes back to save us,' said Job. 'We've been calculating upon his help – otherwise things be as bad as they were before. We three have clung here waiting for death these two hours, and now there's one more to wait for death – unless the shoemaker comes back.'

Job spoke stoically in the face of the cobbler's disappearance, and Steve tried to look cool also; but I think they felt as much discouraged as I, and almost as much as the miller, at the unaccountable vanishing of Cobbler Jones.

On reflection, however, there was no reason to suppose that he had basely deserted us. Probably he had only gone to bring further assistance. But the bare possibility of disappointment at such times is enough to take the nerve from any man or boy.

'He *must* mean to come back!' the miller murmured lugubriously, as we all stood in a row on the ledge, like sparrows on the moulding of a chimney.

'I should think so,' said Steve, 'if he's a man.'

'Yes – he must!' the miller anxiously repeated. 'I once

said he was a twopenny sort of workman to his face – I wish I hadn't said it, oh – how I wish I hadn't; but 'twas years and years ago, and pray heaven he's forgot it! I once called him a stingy varmint – that I did! But we've made that up, and been friends ever since. And yet there's men who'll carry a snub in their buzzoms; and perhaps he's going to punish me now!'

''Twould be very wrong of him,' said I, 'to leave us three to die because you've been a wicked man in your time, miller.'

'Quite true,' said Job.

'Zounds take your saucy tongues!' said Griffin. 'If I had elbow room on this miserable perch I'd – I'd –'

'Just do nothing,' said Job at his elbow. 'Have you no more sense of decency, Mr Griffin, than to go on like that, and the waters rising to drown us minute by minute?'

'Rising to drown us – hey?' said the miller.

'Yes, indeed,' broke in Steve. 'It has reached my feet.'

CHAPTER
5

How we became close allies with the villagers

. . . I floated across to the spot under the opening, when the men all heaved, and I felt myself swinging in the air . . .

Sure enough, the water – to which we had given less attention since the miller's arrival – had kept on rising with silent and pitiless regularity. To feel it actually lapping over the ledge was enough to paralyse us all. We listened and looked, but no shoemaker appeared. In no very long time it ran into our boots, and coldly encircled our ankles.

Miller Griffin trembled so much that he could scarcely keep his standing. 'If I do get out of this,' he said, 'I'll do good – lots of good – to everybody! Oh, oh – the water!'

'Surely you can hold your tongue if this little boy can bear it without crying out!' said Job, alluding to me.

Thus rebuked, the miller was silent; and nothing more happened till we heard a slight sound from the opening which was our only hope, and saw a slight light. We watched, and the light grew stronger, flickering about the orifice like a smile on parted lips. Then hats and heads broke above the edge of the same – one, two, three, four – then candles, arms and shoulders; and it could be seen then that our deliverers were provided with ropes.

'Ahoy – all right!' they shouted, and you may be sure we shouted back a reply.

'Quick, in the name o' goodness!' cried the miller.

A consultation took place among those above, and one of them shouted, 'We'll throw you a rope's end and you must catch it. If you can make it fast, and so climb up one at a time, do it.'

'If not, tie it round the first one, let him jump into the water; we'll tow him across by the rope till he's underneath us, and then haul him up.'

'Yes, yes, that's the way!' said the miller. 'But do be quick – I'm dead drowned up to my thighs. Let me have the rope.'

'Now, miller, that's not fair!' said one of the group above – the Man who had Failed, for he was with them. 'Of course you'll send up the boys first – the little boy first of all.'

'I will – I will – 'twas a mistake,' Griffin replied with contrition.

The rope was then thrown; Job caught it, and tied it round me. It was with some misgiving that I flung myself on the water; but I did it, and, upheld by the rope, I floated across to the spot in the pool that was perpendicularly under the opening, when the men all heaved, and I felt myself swinging in the air, till I was received into the arms of half the parish. For the alarm having been given, the attempt at rescue was known all over the lower part of West Poley.

My cousin Steve was now hauled up. When he had gone the miller burst into a sudden terror at the thought of being left till the last, fearing he might not be able to catch the rope. He implored Job to let him go up first.

'Well,' said Job; 'so you shall – on one condition.'

'Tell it, and I agree.'

Job searched his pockets, and drew out a little floury pocket-book, in which he had been accustomed to enter sales of meal and bran. Without replying to the miller, he stooped to the candle and wrote. This done he said, 'Sign this, and I'll let ye go.'

The miller read: *I hereby certify that I release from this time forth Job Tray, my apprentice, by his wish, and demand no further service from him whatever.* 'Very well – have your way,' he said; and taking the pencil subscribed his name. By this time they had untied Steve and were flinging the rope a third time; Job caught it as before, attached it to the miller's portly person, shoved him off, and saw him hoisted. The dragging up on this occasion was a test to the muscles of those above; but it was accomplished. Then the rope was flung back for the last time, and fortunate it was that the delay was no longer. Job could only manage to secure himself with great difficulty, owing to the numbness which was creeping over him from his heavy labours and immersions. More dead than alive he was pulled to the top with the rest.

The people assembled above began questioning us, as

well they might, upon how we had managed to get into our perilous position. Before we had explained, a gurgling sound was heard from the pool. Several looked over. The water whose rising had nearly caused our death was sinking suddenly; and the light of the candle, which had been left to burn itself out on the ledge, revealed a whirlpool on the surface. Steve, the only one of our trio who was in a condition to observe anything, knew in a moment what the phenomenon meant.

The weight of accumulated water had completed the task of reopening the closed tunnel or fissure which Job's and Steve's diving had begun; and the stream was rushing rapidly down the old West Poley outlet, through which it had run from geological times. In a few minutes – as I was told, for I was not an eyewitness of further events this night – the water had drained itself out, and the stream could be heard trickling across the floor of the lower cave as before the check.

In the explanations which followed our adventure, the following facts were disclosed as to our discovery by the neighbours.

The miller and the shoemaker, after a little further discussion in the road where I overheard them, decided to investigate the caves one by one. With this object in view they got a lantern, and proceeded, not to Nick's Pocket, but to a well-known cave nearer at hand called Grim Billy, which to them seemed a likely source for the river.

This cave was very well known up to a certain point. The floor sloped upwards, and eventually led to the margin of the hole in the dome of Nick's Pocket; but nobody was aware that it was the inner part of Nick's Pocket which the treacherous opening revealed. Rather was the unplumbed depth beneath supposed to be the mouth of an abyss into which no human being could venture. Thus when a stone ascended from this abyss (the stone I threw) the searchers were amazed, till the miller's intuition suggested to him that we were there. And, what was most curious, when we were all delivered, and had gone home, and had been put into warm beds, neither the miller nor the shoemaker knew for certain that they had lighted upon the source of the mill-stream. Much less did they suspect the contrivance we had discovered for turning the water to East or West Poley, at pleasure.

By a piece of good fortune, Steve's mother heard nothing of what had happened to us till we appeared dripping at the door, and could testify to our deliverance before explaining our perils.

The result which might have been expected to all of us, followed in the case of Steve. He caught cold from his prolonged duckings, and the cold was followed by a serious illness.

The illness of Steve was attended with slight fever, which left him very weak, though neither Job nor I suffered any evil effects from our immersion.

The mill-stream having flowed back to its course, the mill was again started, and the miller troubled himself no further about the river-head; but Job, thanks to his ingenuity, was no longer the miller's apprentice. He had been lucky enough to get a place in another mill many miles off, the very next day after our escape.

I frequently visited Steve in his bedroom, and, on one of these occasions, he said to me, 'Suppose I were to die, and you were to go away home, and Job were always to stay away in another part of England, the secret of that mill-stream head would be lost to our village; so that if by chance the vent this way were to choke, and the water run into the East Poley channel, our people would not know how to recover it. They saved our lives, and we ought to make them the handsome return of telling them the whole manœuvre.'

This was quite my way of thinking, and it was decided that Steve should tell all as soon as he was well enough. But I soon found that his anxiety on the matter seriously affected his recovery. He had a scheme, he said, for preventing such a loss of the stream again.

Discovering that Steve was uneasy in his mind, the doctor – to whom I explained that Steve desired to make personal reparation – insisted that his wish be gratified at once – namely, that some of the leading inhabitants of West Poley should be brought up to his bedroom, and learn what he had to say. His mother assented, and messages were sent to them at once.

The villagers were ready enough to come, for they guessed the object of the summons, and they were anxious, too, to know more particulars of our adventures than we had as yet had opportunity to tell them. Accordingly, at a little past six that evening, when the sun was going down, we heard their footsteps ascending the stairs, and they entered. Among them there were the blacksmith, the shoemaker, the dairyman, the Man who had Failed, a couple of farmers; and some men who worked on the farms were also admitted.

Some chairs were brought up from below, and, when our visitors had settled down, Steve's mother, who was very anxious about him, said, 'Now, my boy, we are all here. What have you to tell?'

Steve began at once, explaining first how we had originally discovered the inner cave, and how we walked on till we came to a stream.

'What we want to know is this,' said the shoemaker, 'is that great pool we fetched you out of, the head of the mill-stream?'

Steve explained that it was not a natural pool, and other things which the reader already knows. He then came to the description of the grand manœuvre by which the stream could be turned into either the east or the west valley.

'But how did you get down there?' asked one. 'Did you walk in through Giant's Ear, or Goblin's Cellar, or Grim Billy?'

'We did not enter by either of these,' said Steve. 'We entered by Nick's Pocket.'

'Ha!' said the company, 'that explains all the mystery.'

''Tis amazing,' said the miller, who had entered, 'that folks should have lived and died here for generations, and never ha' found out that Nick's Pocket led to the river spring!'

'Well, that isn't all I want to say,' resumed Steve.

'Suppose any people belonging to East Poley should find out the secret, they would go there and turn the water into their own vale; and, perhaps, close up the other channel in such a way that we could scarcely open it again. But didn't somebody leave the room a minute ago? – who is it that's going away?'

'I fancy a man went out,' said the dairyman looking round. One or two others said the same, but dusk having closed in it was not apparent which of the company had gone away.

Steve continued: 'Therefore before the secret is known, let somebody of our village go and close up the little gallery we entered by, and the upper mouth you looked in from. Then there'll be no danger of our losing the water again.'

The proposal was received with unanimous commendation, and after a little more consultation, and the best wishes of the neighbours for Steve's complete recovery, they took their leave, arranging to go and stop the cave entrances the next evening.

As the doctor had thought, so it happened. No sooner was his sense of responsibility gone, than Steve began to mend with miraculous rapidity. Four and twenty hours made such a difference in him that he said to me, with animation, the next evening: 'Do, Leonard, go and bring me word what they are doing at Nick's Pocket. They ought to be going up there about this time to close up the gallery. But 'tis quite dark – you'll be afraid.'

'No – not I,' I replied, and off I went, having told my aunt my mission.

It was, indeed, quite dark, and it was not till I got quite close to the mill that I found several West Poley men had gathered in the road opposite thereto. The miller was not among them, being too much shaken by his fright for any active enterprise. They had spades, pickaxes, and other tools, and were just preparing for the start to the caves.

I followed behind, and as soon as we reached the outskirts of West Poley, I found they all made straight for Nick's Pocket as planned. Arrived there, they lit their candles and we went into the interior. Though they had been most precisely informed by Steve how to find the connecting gallery with the inner cavern, so cunningly was it hidden by Nature's hand that they probably would have occupied no small time in lighting on it, if I had not gone forward and pointed out the nook.

They thanked me, and the dairyman, as one of the most active of the group, taking a spade in one hand, and a light in the other, prepared to creep in first and foremost. He had not advanced many steps before he reappeared in the outer cave, looking as pale as death.

CHAPTER

6

HOW ALL OUR DIFFICULTIES
CAME TO AN END

*. . . We crept close to the gallery mouth and listened.
'Whoever they call themselves, they are at work like the
busy bee!'*

'WHAT's the matter!' said the shoemaker.

'Somebody's there!' he gasped.

'It can't be,' said a farmer. 'Till those boys found the
hole, not a being in the world knew of such a way in.'

'Well, come and harken for yourselves,' said the dairyman.

We crept close to the gallery mouth and listened. Peck,
peck, peck; scrape, scrape, scrape, could be heard distinctly inside.

'Whoever they call themselves, they are at work like
the busy bee!' said the farmer.

It was ultimately agreed that some of the party should
go softly round into Grim Billy, creep up the ascent
within the cave, and peer through the opening that
looked down through the roof of the cave before us. By

this means they might learn, unobserved, what was going on.

It was no sooner proposed than carried out. The baker and shoemaker were the ones that went round, and, as there was nothing to be seen where the others waited, I thought I would bear them company. To get to Grim Billy, a circuit of considerable extent was necessary; moreover, we had to cross the mill-stream. The mill had been stopped for the night, some time before, and, hence, it was by a pure chance we noticed that the river was gradually draining itself out. The misfortune initiated by Steve was again upon the village.

'I wonder if the miller knows it?' murmured the shoemaker. 'If not, we won't tell him, or he may lose his senses outright.'

'Then the folks in the cave are enemies!' said the farmer.

'True,' said the baker, 'for nobody else can have done this – let's push on.'

Grim Billy being entered, we crawled on our hands and knees up the slope, which eventually terminated at the hole above Nick's Pocket – a hole that probably no human being had passed through before we were hoisted up through it on the evening of our marvellous escape. We were careful to make no noise in ascending, and, at the edge, we gazed cautiously over.

A striking sight met our view. A number of East Poley men were assembled on the floor, which had been for awhile submerged by our exploit; and they were working with all their might to build and close up the old outlet of the stream towards West Poley, having already, as it appeared, opened the new opening towards their own village, discovered by Steve. We understood it in a moment, and, descending with the same softness as before, we returned to where our comrades were waiting for us in the other cave, where we told them the strange sight we had seen.

'How did they find out the secret?' the shoemaker inquired under his breath. 'We have guarded it as we would ha' guarded our lives.'

'I can guess!' replied the baker. 'Have you forgot how somebody went away from Master Steve Draycot's bedroom in the dusk last night, and we didn't know who it was? Half an hour after, such a man was seen crossing the hill to East Poley; I was told so today. We've been surprised, and must hold our own by main force, since we can no longer do it by stealth.'

'How, main force?' asked the blacksmith and a farmer simultaneously.

'By closing the gallery they went in by,' said the baker. 'Then we shall have them in prison, and bring them to book rarely.'

The rest being all irritated at having been circumvented so slyly and selfishly by the East Poley men, the baker's plan met with ready acceptance. Five of our body at once chose hard boulders from the outer cave, of such a bulk that they would roll about half-way into the passage or gallery – where there was a slight enlargement – but which would pass no farther. These being put in position, they were easily wedged there, and it was impossible to remove them from within, owing to the diminishing size of the passage, except by more powerful tools than they had, which were only spades. We now felt sure of our antagonists, and in a far better position to argue with them than if they had been free. No longer taking the trouble to preserve silence, we, of West Poley, walked in a body round to the other cave – Grim Billy – ascended the inclined floor like a flock of goats, and arranged ourselves in a group at the opening that impended over Nick's Pocket.

The East Poley men were still working on, absorbed in their labour, and were unconscious that twenty eyes regarded them from above like stars.

'Let's halloo!' said the baker.

Halloo we did with such vigour that the East Poley

men, taken absolutely unawares, wellnigh sprang into the air at the shock it produced on their nerves. Their spades flew from their hands, and they stared around in dire alarm, for the echoes confused them as to the direction whence the hallooing came. They finally turned their eyes upwards, and saw us individuals of the rival village far above them, illuminated with candles, and with countenances grave and stern as a bench of unmerciful judges.

'Men of East Poley,' said the baker, 'we have caught ye in the execution of a most unfair piece of work. Because of a temporary turning of our water into your vale by a couple of meddlesome boys – a piece of mischief that was speedily repaired – you have thought fit to covet our stream. You have sent a spy to find out its secret, and have meanfully come here to steal the stream for yourselves for ever. This cavern is in our parish, and you have no right here at all.'

'The waters of the earth be as much ours as yours,' said one from beneath. But the remainder were thunderstruck, for they knew that their chance had lain entirely in strategy and not in argument.

The shoemaker then spoke: 'Ye have entered upon our property, and diverted the water, and made our parish mill useless, and caused us other losses. Do ye agree to restore it to its old course, close up the new course ye have been at such labour to widen – in short, to leave things as they have been from time immemorial?'

'No-o-o-o!' was shouted from below in a yell of defiance.

'Very well, then,' said the baker, 'we must make you. Gentlemen, ye are prisoners. Until you restore that water to us, you will bide where you be.'

The East Poley men rushed to escape by the way they had entered. But half-way up the tunnel a barricade of adamantine blocks barred their footsteps. 'Bring spades!' shouted the foremost. But the stones were so well wedged, and the passage so small, that, as we had anticipated, no engineering force at their disposal could make the least impression upon the blocks. They returned to the inner cave disconsolately.

'D'ye give in?' we asked them.

'Never!' said they doggedly.

'Let 'em sweat – let 'em sweat,' said the shoemaker, placidly. 'They'll tell a different tale by tomorrow morning. Let 'em bide for the night, and say no more.'

In pursuance of this idea we withdrew from our position, and, passing out of Grim Billy, went straight home. Steve was excited by the length of my stay, and still more when I told him the cause of it. 'What – got them prisoners in the cave?' he said. 'I must go myself tomorrow and see the end of this!'

Whether it was partly due to the excitement of the occasion, or solely to the recuperative powers of a strong constitution, cannot be said; but certain it is that next morning, on hearing the villagers shouting and gathering together, Steve sprang out of bed, declaring that he must go with me to see what was happening to the prisoners. The doctor was hastily called in, and gave it as his opinion that the outing would do Steve no harm, if he were warmly wrapped up; and soon away we went, just in time to overtake the men who had started on their way.

With breathless curiosity we entered Grim Billy, lit our candles and clambered up the incline. Almost before we reached the top, exclamations ascended through the chasm to Nick's Pocket, there being such words as, 'We give in!' 'Let us out!' 'We give up the water for ever!'

Looking in upon them, we found their aspect to be very different from what it had been the night before. Some had extemporized a couch with smock-frocks and gaiters, and jumped up from a sound sleep thereon; while others had their spades in their hands, as if undoing what they had been at such pains to build up, as was proved in a moment by their saying eagerly, 'We have begun to put it right, and shall finish soon – we are restoring the river to his old bed – give us your word, good gentlemen, that when it is done we shall be free!'

'Certainly,' replied our side with great dignity. 'We have said so already.'

Our arrival stimulated them in the work of repair, which had hitherto been somewhat desultory. Then shovels entered the clay and rubble like giants' tongues; they lit up more candles, and in half an hour had completely demolished the structure raised the night before with such labour and amazing solidity that it might have been expected to last for ever. The final stone rolled away, the much tantalized river withrew its last drop from the new channel, and resumed its original course once more.

While the East Poley men had been completing this task, some of our party had gone back to Nick's Pocket, and there, after much exertion, succeeded in unpacking the boulders from the horizontal passage admitting to the inner cave. By the time this was done, the prisoners within had finished their work of penance, and we West Poley men, who had remained to watch them, rejoined our companions. Then we all stood back, while those of East Poley came out, walking between their vanquishers, like the Romans under the Caudine Forks, when they surrendered to the Samnites. They glared at us with suppressed rage, and passed without saying a word.

'I see from their manner that we have not heard the last of this,' said the Man who had Failed, thoughtfully. He had just joined us, and learnt the state of the case.

'I was thinking as much,' said the shoemaker. 'As long as that cave is known in Poley, so long will they bother us about the stream.'

'I wish it had never been found out,' said the baker bitterly. 'If not now upon us, they will be playing that trick upon our children when we are dead and gone.'

Steve glanced at me, and there was sadness in his look.

We walked home considerably in the rear of the rest, by no means at ease. It was impossible to disguise from ourselves that Steve had lost the good feeling of his fellow parishioners by his explorations and their results.

As the West Poley men had predicted, so it turned out. Some months afterwards, when I had gone back to my home and school, and Steve was learning to superintend his mother's farm, I heard that another midnight entry had been made into the cave by the rougher characters of East Poley. They diverted the stream as before, and when the miller and other inhabitants of the West village rose in the morning, behold, their stream was dry! The West Poley folk were furious, and rushed to Nick's Pocket. The mischief-makers were gone, and there was no legal proof as to their identity, though it was indirectly clear enough where they had come from. With some difficulty the water was again restored, but not till Steve had again been spoken of as the original cause of the misfortunes.

About this time I paid another visit to my cousin and aunt. Steve seemed to have grown a good deal older than when I had last seen him, and, almost as soon as we were alone, he began to speak on the subject of the mill-stream.

'I am glad you have come, Leonard,' he said, 'for I want to talk to you. I have never been happy, you know, since the adventure; I don't like the idea that by a freak of mine our village should be placed at the mercy of the East Poleyites; I shall never be liked again unless I make that river as secure from interruption as it was before.'

'But that can't be,' said I.

'Well, I have a scheme,' said Steve musingly. 'I am not so sure that the river may not be made as secure as it was before.'

'But how? What is the scheme based on?' I asked, incredulously.

'I cannot reveal to you at present,' said he. 'All I can say is, that I have injured my native village, that I owe it amends, and that I'll pay the debt if it's a possibility.'

I soon perceived from my cousin's manner at meals and elsewhere that the scheme, whatever it might be, occupied him to the exclusion of all other thoughts. But he would not speak to me about it. I frequently missed him for spaces of an hour or two, and soon conjectured that these hours of absence were spent in furtherance of his plan.

The last day of my visit came round, and to tell the truth I was not sorry, for Steve was so preoccupied as to be anything but a pleasant companion. I walked up to the village alone, and soon became aware that something had happened.

During the night another raid had been made upon the river-head – with but partial success, it is true; but the stream was so much reduced that the mill-wheel would not turn, and the dipping pools were nearly empty. It was resolved to repair the mischief in the evening, but the disturbance in the village was very great, for the attempt proved that the more unscrupulous characters of East Poley were not inclined to desist.

Before I had gone much farther, I was surprised to discern in the distance a figure which seemed to be Steve's, though I thought I had left him at the rear of his mother's premises.

He was making for Nick's Pocket, and following thither I reached the mouth of the cave just in time to see him enter.

'Steve!' I called out. He heard me and came back. He was pale, and there seemed to be something in his face which I had never seen there before.

'Ah – Leonard,' he said, 'you have traced me. Well, you are just in time. The folks think of coming to mend this mischief as soon as their day's work is over, but perhaps it won't be necessary. My scheme may do instead.'

'How – do instead?' asked I.

'Well, save them the trouble,' he said with assumed carelessness. 'I had almost decided not to carry it out, though I have got the materials in readiness, but the doings of the night have stung me; I carry out my plan.'

'When?'

'Now – this hour – this moment. The stream must flow into its right channel, and stay there, and no man's hands must be able to turn it elsewhere. Now good-bye, in case of accidents.'

To my surprise, Steve shook hands with me solemnly, and wringing from me a promise not to follow, disappeared into the blackness of the cave.

For some moments I stood motionless where Steve had left me, not quite knowing what to do. Hearing footsteps behind my back, I looked round. To my great pleasure I saw Job approaching, dressed up in his best clothes, and with him the Man who had Failed.

Job was glad to see me. He had come to West Poley for a holiday, from the situation with the farmer which, as I now learned for the first time, the Man who had Failed had been the means of his obtaining. Observing, I suppose, the perplexity upon my face, they asked me what was the matter, and I, after some hesitation, told them of Steve. The Man who had Failed looked grave.

'Is it serious?' I asked him.

'It may be,' said he, in that poetico-philosophic strain which, under more favouring circumstances, might have led him on to the intellectual eminence of a Coleridge or an Emerson. 'Your cousin, like all such natures, is rushing into another extreme, that may be worse than the first. The opposite of error is error still; from careless adventuring at other people's expense he may have flown to rash self-sacrifice. He contemplates some violent remedy, I make no doubt. How long has he been in the cave? We had better follow him.'

Before I could reply, we were startled by a jet of smoke, like that from the muzzle of a gun, bursting from the mouth of Nick's Pocket; and this was immediately followed by a deadened rumble like thunder underground. In another moment a duplicate of the noise reached our ears from over the hill, in the precise direction of Grim Billy.

'Oh – what can it be?' said I.

'Gunpowder,' said the Man who had Failed, slowly.

'Ah – yes – I know what he's done – he has blasted the rock inside!' cried Job. 'Depend upon it, that's his plan for closing up the way to the river-head.'

'And for losing his life into the bargain,' said our companion. 'But no – he may be alive. We must go in at once – or as soon as we can breathe there.'

Job ran for lights, and before he returned we heard a familiar sound from the direction of the village. It was the patter of the mill-wheel. Job came up almost at the moment, and with him a crowd of the village people.

'The river is right again,' they shouted. 'Water runs better than ever – a full, steady stream, all on a sudden – just when we heard the rumble underground.'

'Steve has done it!' I said.

'A brave fellow,' said the Man who had Failed. 'Pray that he is not hurt.'

Job had lighted the candles, and, when we were entering, some more villagers, who at the noise of the explosion had run to Grim Billy, joined us. 'Grim Billy is partly closed up inside!' they told us. 'Where you used to climb up the slope to look over into Nick's Pocket, 'tis all altered. There's no longer any opening there; the whole rock has crumbled down as if the mountain had sunk bodily.'

Without waiting to answer, we, who were about to enter Nick's Pocket, proceeded on our way. We soon had penetrated to the outer approaches, though nearly suffocated by the sulphurous atmosphere; but we could get no farther than the first cavern. At a point somewhat in advance of the little gallery to the inner cave, Nick's Pocket ceased to exist. Its roof had sunk. The whole superimposed mountain, as it seemed, had quietly settled down upon the hollow places beneath it, closing like a pair of bellows, and barring all human entrance.

But alas, where was Steve? 'I would liever have had no water in West Poley for ever more than have lost Steve!' said Job.

'And so would I!' said many of us.

To add to our terror, news was brought into the cave at that moment that Steve's mother was approaching; and

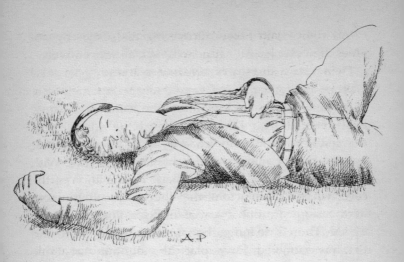

how to meet my poor aunt was more than we could think.

But suddenly a shout was heard. A few of the party, who had not penetrated so far into the cave as we had done, were exclaiming, 'Here he is!' We hastened back, and found they were in a small, side hollow, close to the entrance, which we had passed by unheeded. The Man who had Failed was there, and he and the baker were carrying something into the light. It was Steve – apparently dead, or unconscious.

'Don't be frightened,' said the baker to me. 'He's not dead; perhaps not much hurt.'

As he had declared, so it turned out. No sooner was Steve in the open air, then he unclosed his eyes, looked round with a stupefied expression, and sat up.

'Steve – Steve!' said Job and I, simultaneously.

'All right,' said Steve, recovering his senses by degrees. 'I'll tell – how it happened – in a minute or two.'

Then his mother came up, and was at first terrified enough, but on seeing Steve gradually get upon his legs, she recovered her equanimity. He soon was able to explain all. He said that the damage to the village by his tampering with the stream had weighed upon his mind, and led him to revolve many schemes for its cure. With this in view he had privately made examination of the cave; when he discovered that the whole superincumbent mass, forming the roof of the inner cave, was divided from the walls of the same by a vein of sand, and that it was only kept in its place by a slim support at one corner. It seemed to him that if this support could be removed, the upper mass would descend by its own weight, like the brick of a brick-trap when the peg is withdrawn.

He laid his plans accordingly; procuring gunpowder, and scooping out holes for the same, at central points in the rock. When all this was done, he waited a while, in doubt, as to the effect; and might possibly never have completed his labours, but for the renewed attempt upon the river. He then made up his mind, and attached the fuse. After lighting it, he would have reached the outside safely enough but for the accident of stumbling as he ran, which threw him so heavily to the ground, that, before he could recover himself and go forward, the explosion had occurred.

All of us congratulated him, and the whole village was joyful, for no less than three thousand, four hundred and fifty tons of rock and earth – according to calculations made by an experienced engineer a short time afterwards – had descended between the river's head and all human interference, so that there was not much fear of any more East Poley manœuvres for turning the stream into their valley.

The inhabitants of the parish, gentle and simple, said that Steve had made ample amends for the harm he had done; and their goodwill was further evidenced by his being invited to no less than nineteen Christmas and New Year's parties during the following holidays.

As we left the cave, Steve, Job, Mrs Draycot and I walked behind the Man who had Failed.

'Though this has worked well,' he said to Steve, 'it is by the merest chance in the world. Your courage is praiseworthy, but you see the risks that are incurred when people go out of their way to meddle with what they don't understand. Exceptionally smart actions, such as you delight in, should be carefully weighed with a view to their utility before they are begun. Quiet perseverance in clearly defined courses is, as a rule, better than the erratic exploits that may do much harm.'

Steve listened respectfully enough to this, but he said to his mother afterwards, 'He has failed in life, and how can his opinions be worth anything?'

'For this reason,' said she. 'He is one who has failed, not from want of sense, but from want of energy; and people of that sort, when kindly, are better worth attending to than those successful ones, who have never seen the seamy side of things. I would advise you to listen to him.'

Steve probably did; for he is now the largest gentleman-farmer of those parts, remarkable for his avoidance of anything like speculative exploits.